Library of Congress Cataloging-in-Publication Data
Yeoman, John.
Old Mother Hubbard's dog needs a doctor / John Yeoman and
Quentin Blake.—1st American ed.
p.   cm.
Summary: Old Mother Hubbard's dog feigns a series of
illnesses to escape the threat of taking some exercise.
ISBN 0-395-53359-7
[1. Dogs—Fiction. 2. Stories in rhyme.] I. Blake, Quentin.
II. Title.
PZ8.3.Y4601 1990   89-24448
[E]—dc20   CIP
                                                        AC

Text copyright © 1989 by John Yeoman
Illustrations copyright © 1989 by Quentin Blake
First American edition 1990
Originally published in Great Britain in 1989
by Walker Books Ltd.

Printed in Italy.
10 9 8 7 6 5 4 3 2 1

Old Mother Hubbard's Dog

Needs a Doctor

John Yeoman & Quentin Blake

Houghton Mifflin Company
Boston 1990

Said Old Mother Hubbard one fine afternoon,
Preparing to polish the bell,
"You ought to be taking some exercise soon:
You're really not looking too well."

And while she was dusting and sweeping the floor
And shining the pans and the pots,
The dog found some paint tins behind the back door
And covered himself in bright spots.

She made a strong soup, using carrots and peas
And turnips and onions and such,
Thinking, "This ought to cure him of any disease."
But the dog hopped away on a crutch.

He reappeared, causing his mistress to stare,
And tremble, and turn very pale:
He was bowling along in an invalid chair
And was bandaged from whiskers to tail.

He then had the hiccups, which frightened the cat,
And made all the window frames shake.
Said Old Mother Hubbard, "I'm not standing that:
My head is beginning to ache."

The dog looked quite sorry, and took to his bed;
She saw his tears starting to form.
She gave him a large block of ice for his head
And bedsocks to keep his feet warm.

She knew that there wasn't a moment to lose;
She saddled her pig in the sty.
She went for the doctor. He couldn't refuse:
Her poor little dog mustn't die.

They trotted back slowly (the pig wouldn't run);
She felt much too anxious to talk.
But there was her dog, doing handsprings for fun,
Before setting off for a walk.